Woodbourne Library
Washington-Centerville Public Library
Centerville, Ohio

DISCARD

W9-AFM-507

A big, very big thank you to you, Jean.
There will always be a flower for you in my books.

Text and illustrations © 2013 Éditions Milan

Published in North America in 2014 by Owlkids Books Inc.

Published in France under the title *Le petit oiseau va sortir* in 2013 by Éditions Milan

All rights reserved. No part of this publication may be reproduced, stored in a retrieval system, or transmitted in any form or by any means, without the prior written permission of Owlkids Books Inc., or in the case of photocopying or other reprographic copying, a license from the Canadian Copyright Licensing Agency (Access Copyright). For an Access Copyright license, visit www.accesscopyright.ca or call toll-free to 1-800-893-5777.

Owlkids Books acknowledges the financial support of the Canada Council for the Arts, the Ontario Arts Council, the Government of Canada through the Canada Book Fund (CBF) and the Government of Ontario through the Ontario Media Development Corporation's Book Initiative for our publishing activities.

Published in Canada by	Published in the United States by
Owlkids Books Inc.	Owlkids Books Inc.
10 Lower Spadina Avenue	1700 Fourth Street
Toronto, ON M5V 2Z2	Berkeley, CA 94710

Library and Archives Canada Cataloguing in Publication

Manceau, Édouard, 1969- [Petit oiseau va sortir. English]
    Hatch, little egg / Édouard Manceau ; translated by Karen Li.

Translation of: Le petit oiseau va sortir ....
ISBN 978-1-77147-077-3 (bound)

    I. Li, Karen, translator II. Title. III. Title: Petit oiseau va sortir. English.

PZ7.M333Ha 2014   j843'.92   C2014-900393-5

Library of Congress Control Number: 2014932280

Manufactured in Shenzhen, Guangdong, China, in March 2014, by WKT Co. Ltd.
Job #13B2749

A   B   C   D   E   F

Owl kids Publisher of Chirp, chickaDEE and OWL
www.owlkidsbooks.com

Édouard Manceau

HATCH, LITTLE EGG

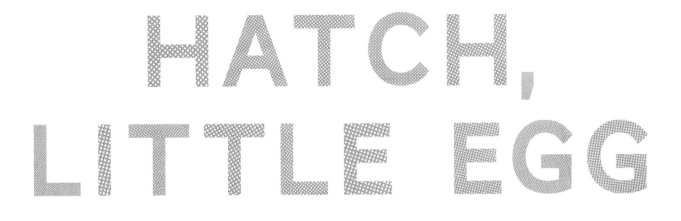

"Hey, Jack! Are you going to see the little bird hatch?"
"That's what I wanted to do, but my car broke down."
"No problem. Hop on my motorcycle."
"You're going, too?"
"Of course!"

"Look! Everyone's going..."
"It's all anyone is talking about!"

"The little bird is hatching!"
"The little bird is hatching!"

"Come on! This way!"

"Look! There it is!"
"Quick! Quick! Over here!"

"Ooooh! Here we go!"
"Hatch, little egg!"
"Get ready! One, two, three…"

"Ohhhhhhh!!!"
"What on earth...?"

"What? You've never seen a pig before?
Don't you want to take my picture?"

"Unbelievable! If I hadn't seen it with my own eyes!"
"I know! It's crazy!"
"Tell me about it!"
"Oh, I am so, so, so disappointed..."
"Me, too! Who does that pig think he is?"

"Honestly, what's the big deal? You can't even hatch in peace these days! But...

...at least I did it my way!"